Dear Kyle & Chloe
This book was illustrated by a friend of mine. She washes my hair when I go to have it cut. I bought this book for you both to share the delightful story.
                                    I love you, Mimi 2012

Santa will ALWAYS find You because at your WONDERFUL HEART!
                        Jordan Jordan 12/14/12

Dear Kyle and Chloe
Where ever you are
Wherever you go... enjoy the
Magic of Christmas
Nancy LeBlanc

THE Santa Beacon

This special book belongs especially to...

_____

THE Santa Beacon

Written by Graham Gardner
Illustrated by Nancy LeBlanc

BELLE ISLE BOOKS
www.belleislebooks.com

ISBN: 978-0-9859358-0-1

Library of Congress Control Number: 2012913248

Published by

BELLE ISLE BOOKS
www.belleislebooks.com

To Ava, Finn, and Oliver...
Please listen to your mother.

Ava sat straight up in bed. It was six o'clock in the morning on Christmas Eve.

This would be Ava's first Christmas away from home.
She and her parents and brothers were going to spend Christmas at
her grandparents' house. Ava was so excited to see her Grandmart and
Pop-Pop and all her fun cousins.
Ava suddenly realized...
How would Santa find her?

She was going to her Grandmart's and Pop-Pop's house and she had not told Santa that she would not be home!

2

She asked her Uncle Martin about Santa and beacons and where she could find one. Uncle Martin was a sailor, and he said, "Lots of ships have beacons. Sailors use beacons to find their way in the ocean." But there were no ships near Grandmart's and Pop-Pop's house. Uncle Martin did not have a beacon either.

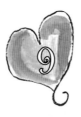

Ava only had a couple of hours to go before bedtime. She started making toys for her brothers so they would have some presents to open in the morning. She tried to make some toys that they would like. Velma helped, but they did not look very much like what Ava had planned.

Pop Pops Workshop

10

After everyone
was asleep, Ava
crept downstairs to
hide her brothers'
presents under
the tree. She cried
a little tear. Ava
knew that Christmas
was about more
than presents, but
she thought her
brothers might not
understand if Santa
didn't come.

11

Suddenly there was a thud in the fireplace
and a jolly laugh. Ava turned to see Santa
Claus with a big sack of toys. Ava and
Velma were very surprised.

"Santa! You came!" exclaimed Ava.

"Of course I came, Ava," Santa said. "But why are you crying?"

"Because I didn't think you knew where we were. How did you find us?"asked Ava.

"That's easy. I used the Santa Beacon," said Santa.

"That's what Uncle Russel said! But we don't have a Santa beacon."

"It's your **heart**, child.
If a child's heart
is good, I can find
them anywhere. And
you have a wonderful
heart, Ava."

"I do?" asked
Ava, "How does it
work, Santa?"

15

Santa explained, "Your heart is as bright as Rudolph's nose and I can see that. It beats as loud as reindeer hoofs on a tin roof, and Mrs. Claus can hear that. She told me where to find you. Thank you for being good, Ava. Now off to bed with you."

Then Santa patted Ava on her head and she suddenly felt very sleepy.

"Thank you, Santa, I want to be good.
Merry Christmas, Santa," said Ava with a big yawn
as she went up the stairs to her bed.
"Pleasant dreams, sweet child," said Santa.

The next day, Ava and her family had a wonderful Christmas. Her brothers loved the toys that Ava made, although they did not know what they were.

Touch your heart ornament every day as a reminder to be good and to be nice to others.

Share kind thoughts with your ornament to build up your heart's power.

For a fun Christmas game, hide your ornament in different places on your Christmas tree and let others try to find it.

And no matter where you are...
Have a **wonderful** Christmas!

THE END

Go back and find the hidden letters on each page to spell out a secret message!

Graham Gardner

Graham was born in West Berlin on an American army base, grew up in a beautiful little town called Martinsville, Virginia, and now lives in Richmond, Virginia with his family in a very strange house on the river. He received his degree in dentistry at Virginia Commonwealth University, and became an orthodontist at New York University, so he gets to help people with their smiles every day. Graham loves spending time with his family, kite boarding and whitewater kayaking but most of all, he loves life! Graham is also published in orthodontic scientific publications, where he writes about the importance of having a great smile. He hopes this book will make you smile, too!

Nancy Cecere-LeBlanc

Nancy LeBlanc was born and grew up in New Jersey and studied art therapy and art education. While volunteering, working odd jobs and raising her children, she has continued to work on her art in a variety of ways, including painting walls and furniture, and making jewelry. Two things have always remained constant in Nancy's life, and that is her love of animals and her love of art. For many years, she has volunteered with a local canine rescue organization, which continues to inspire her work. She now paints pet portraits and works on her own studies of farm animals and other things that spark her fancy. She currently lives in Henrico, Virginia with her husband, three children and various animals.

Ava Gardner

Ava is a beautiful little girl with a big and wonderful heart. She is an awesome rock climber and is much smarter than her dad. Hopefully she does not know this yet. Ava also likes to make people smile, except sometimes her brothers. She has a bear named Panda and two dogs one named Mathilda and the other named Velma. Ava has a beautiful heart because she cares.